TWO LITTLE TRAINS

by Margaret Wise Brown

pictures by Leo and Diane Dillon

HarperCollins Publishers

To Antonia Markiet, Albert Cetta, and John Vitale

— Leo and Diane Dillon

TWO LITTLE TRAINS

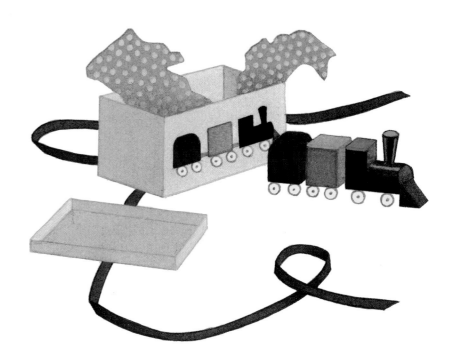

**Two little trains went down the track,
Two little trains went West.**

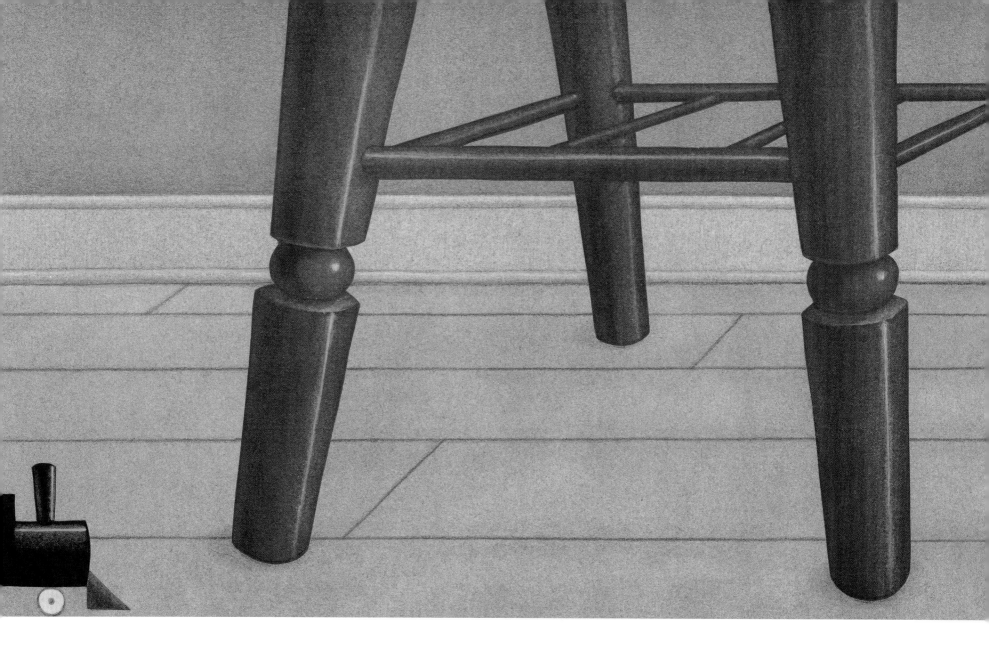

Puff, Puff, Puff and Chug, Chug, Chug,
Two little trains to the West.

**One little train was a streamlined train,
Puff, Puff, Puff to the West.**

**One little train was a little old train,
Chug, Chug, Chug going West.**

**Look down, look down
That long steel track,**

**That long steel track
To the West.**

**Two little trains came to a hill,
A mountainous hill to the West.**

With a Puff and a Chug, they went right through,
Under the hill to the West.

**Look through, look through
That long dark hill,**

That long dark hill
To the West.

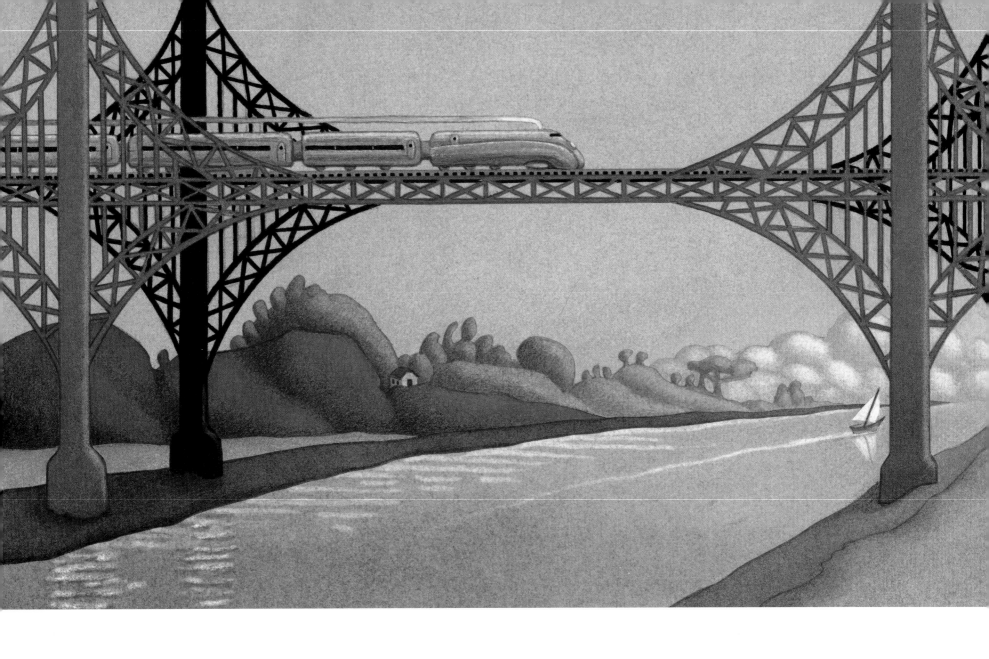

Two little trains came to a river,
Came to a river going West.

With a Puff, Puff, Puff and a Chug, Chug, Chug,
They went over the river to the West.

**Look down, look down
Below the bridge,**

**At the deep dark river
Going West.**

**The rain came down on the two little trains,
On the two little trains going West,**

**And it made them darker, and wet and shiny,
As they went on their way to the West.**

**The snow came down
And covered the ground,
And the two little trains going West.**

And they got white and furry,
And still in a hurry
They puffed and chugged to the West.

The moon shone down on a gleaming track,
And the two little trains going West;

**And they hurried along and heard the song
Of a black man singing in the West.**

**Look down, look down that long steel track
Where you and I must go;**

**That long steel track and strong cross bars,
Before we travel home.**

**The wind it blew, and the dust it flew
Around the two little trains going West.**

**But the dust storm drew not a toot or a whoo
Or a whistle from the trains going West.**

Then the mountains came beyond the plain,
And the trains started climbing West,

**Up and around and over and through
The great high mountains to the West.**

The ocean was big,
The ocean was blue,
Beyond the land in the West.

And the little trains stopped.
Their trip was through.
They had come to the edge of the West.

Library of Congress Cataloging-in-Publication Data

Brown, Margaret Wise.

 Two little trains / by Margaret Wise Brown ; pictures by Leo and Diane Dillon.

      p.   cm.

 Summary: Two little trains, one streamlined, the other old-fashioned, puff, puff, puff, and chug, chug, chug,

on their way West.

 ISBN 0-06-028376-9 — ISBN 0-06-028377-7 (lib. bdg.) — ISBN 0-06-443568-7 (pbk.)

 [1. Railroads—Trains—Fiction.]   I. Dillon, Leo, ill.   II. Dillon, Diane, ill.   III. Title.

PZ7.B8163 Tw   2001   00-40798

[E]—dc21

Typography by Al Cetta

10   11   12   13   SCP   10

First Edition